For my wife Lucy
P.B.

For Joan
J.F.

First
published 2012
by Macmillan Children's Books
This edition published 2021 by Macmillan
Children's Books an imprint of Pan Macmillan
The Smithson, 6 Briset Street,
London, EC1M 5NR
Associated companies
throughout the world
www.panmacmillan.com

ISBN (PB): 9781529016086

The rights of Peter Bently and Jim Field
to be identified as the author and
illustrator of this work have been
asserted in accordance with
the Copyright, Designs
and Patents Act of 1988.

1 3 5 7 9 8 6 4 2

A CIP catalogue record for this book is available from the British Library. Printed in China.

MIX
Paper from
responsible sources
FSC® C116313
FSC
www.fsc.org

PETER BENTLY ★ JIM FIELD

FARMER CLEGG'S ♪♪ NIGHT ♪♪♪ OUT

MACMILLAN CHILDREN'S BOOKS

Out with the dentures, out with the light,
Old Farmer Clegg was tucked up for the night.
The farm was all quiet. No sound could be heard.
Nothing was stirring. Not even a bird.

But wait ... what's that whispering?
That grunting and snuffling?
Up there by the sheep field –
What's shifting and shuffling?

"Quick!" bleated Woolworth, the sheep on the gate.
"The show starts at midnight! Roll up! Don't be late!
We've got some top talent lined up on the show.
Who'll be the winner tonight? We'll soon know!"

TRACTOR
FACTOR
TALENT CONTEST
THE GREATEST SHOW
THIS SIDE OF THE FENCE
COME ONE AND ALL
FEATHERS, WINGS & HOOVES!
SHOW STARTS @ MIDNIGHT

PLEASE
CLOSE
GATE

TRACTOR
FACTOR
TALENT CONTEST
THE GREATEST SHOW
THIS SIDE OF THE FENCE
COME ONE AND ALL
FEATHERS, WINGS & HOOVES!
SHOW STARTS @ MIDNIGHT

First, Dubbin' Dobbin was up on his hooves,
Bustin' some moves to those cool clip-clop grooves.

He spins on his head and he slides on his knees ...

Whoa! What a windmill!

Check out that freeze!

"Next," exclaimed Woolworth, "they're all going bonkers
For Ol' Hissing Hank and his Honky-Tonk Honkers!
Their jazz has pizzazz you can never feel blue to.
These guys are the geese you can never say boo to!"

Then Hettie the Hoofer, the tap-dancing cow,
Cause cries of "Incredible!", "Knockout!" and "Wow!"

She shuffled and scuffled and then did the splits.
It was udderly stunning. They loved her to bits!

"Where's Josey the Juggler?" frowned Simon the judge.
"I've nudged her," said Woolworth. "She simply won't budge!"
"No problem!" said Simon. "Let's keep up the pace.
Who's coming next in this barnstorming race?"

PIG MARIACHI

"It's loco!" cried Woolworth. "It's crazy! It's catchy..."

Then Ramsey and Ramsden, the pop-singer twins!
What singing! What dancing! What cracking great grins!

Their dancing's disastrous. They can't sing a note.
But they sure win full marks in the comedy vote!

Next, silence for Meg, who's the last on the list.
For classical fans this was not to be missed!

The crowd were enchanted as musical Meg
Sang an aria by Mozart while laying an egg.

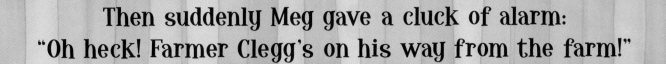
Then suddenly Meg gave a cluck of alarm:
"Oh heck! Farmer Clegg's on his way from the farm!"

"There's no need to panic!" cried Woolworth the sheep.
"Just look at Old Cleggie! He's still fast asleep!"

The animals watched as,
in spite of his age,

The sleepwalking farmer
leapt onto the stage

And in his pyjamas
set off on a jig ...

Then did a few cartwheels
and jived with a pig.

His jigging and jiving had everyone clapping,
With hooves, claws and trotters all merrily tapping.

As Old Farmer Clegg danced a quick tarantella,
The crowd cried, "He's cool! What a brilliant fella!"

"What larks!" Woolworth cried. "What an evening of fun!
Now let's ask the judges to tell us who's won!"

"Right, folks!" declared Simon. "The votes are all in.
It's been really tough working out who should win.

Third place is... Dobbin! Second is... Meg!
But the winner tonight, folks, is...

"Old Farmer Clegg!"

"Hooray for Old Cleggie!" The cheers of delight
Rang out from the audience into the night.

They gave Clegg his trophy as, deeply in slumber,
He strummed air-guitar to a rock 'n' roll number.
Then he flipped off the stage to a roll of the drum...

And sleepwalked back home the same way he had come.

While the crowd were still cheering, the cock started crowing.
"Uh oh," declared Woolworth, "It's time we were going!"

With whispers of "Night-night!"
and "See You!" and "Bye!"
They all hurried homeward to
barn, stall and sty.

As the pink rays of morning crept over the farm,
Old Farmer Clegg switched off his alarm.

In with the dentures, on with the light.
"Ho hum," yawned the farmer. "Another quiet night!"

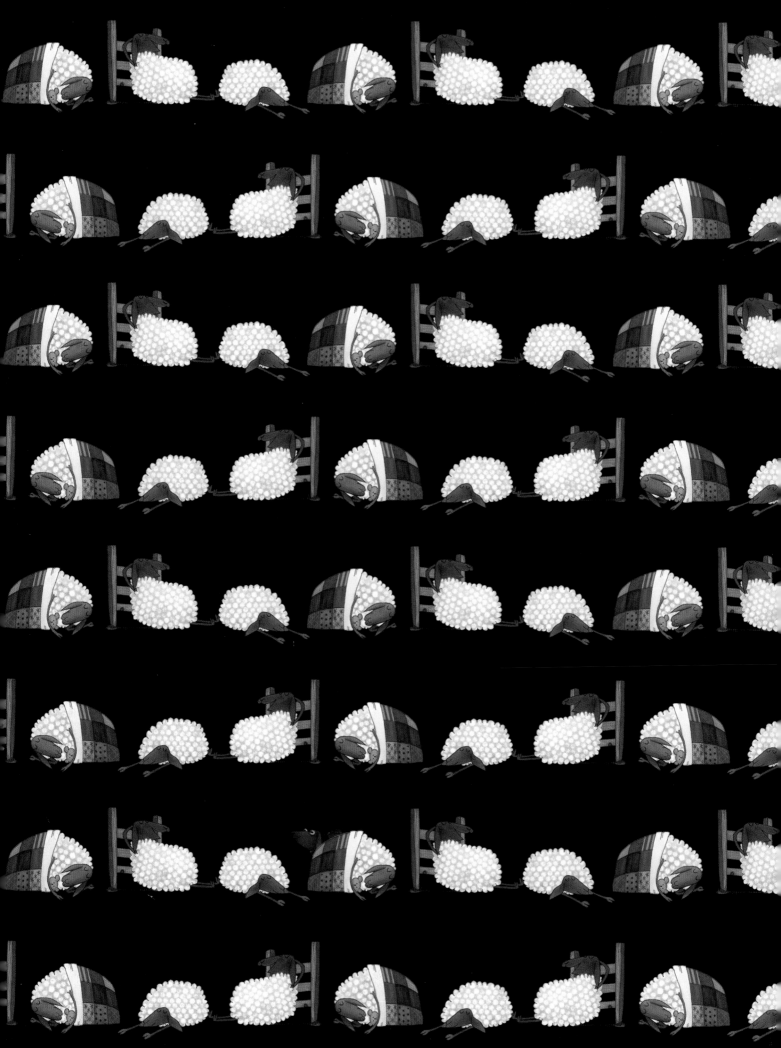

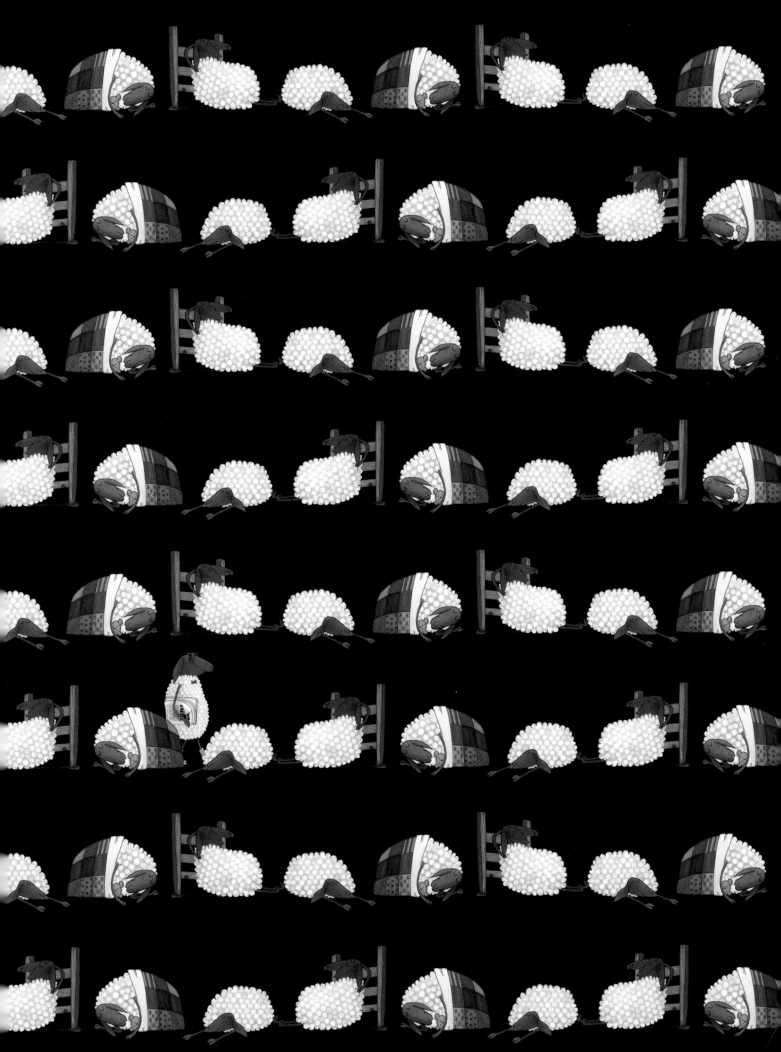